A Big Surprise

Don't miss any of the *paw*fectly fun
books in the **PET HOTEL** series!

PET HOTEL

A Big Surprise

by Kate Finch

illustrated by
John Steven Gurney

SCHOLASTIC INC.

Special thanks to Jane Clarke

For Ruth and Paul, who always make their guests feel welcome.

ISBN 978-0-545-50182-8

Text copyright © 2013 by Working Partners Limited
Cover and interior art copyright © 2013 by Scholastic Inc.

All rights reserved. Published by Scholastic Inc., 557 Broadway, New York, NY 10012, by arrangement with Working Partners Limited. Series created by Working Partners Limited, London.

12 11 10 9 8 7 6 5   14 15 16 17 18/0

Printed in the U.S.A.   40
First printing, July 2013

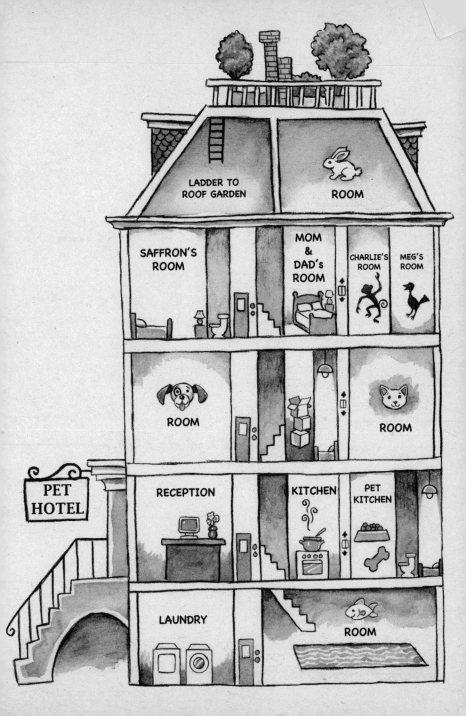

CHAPTER 1

As the sun rose higher in the sky, Gazebo Square echoed with cheerful cries of "Good morning!"

People behind the booths were setting out their brightly colored displays as they greeted their first customers of the day. The square was buzzing with happy chatter, and the air smelled like coffee and freshly baked cinnamon buns. Over at the gazebo bandstand, three boys were playing a happy tune.

"Good morning!" eight-year-old twins Meg and Charlie shouted to their friends as they hurried past. Charlie's backpack was full of yummy breakfast treats. Meg was clutching the handle of a big straw basket in one hand and a dog leash in the other. At the end of the leash was a fluffy golden puppy with a brown marking around one eye, like a pirate's eye patch. Meg smiled proudly. Buster looked so cute prancing along on his big puppy paws.

"Woof!" Buster suddenly barked and tugged his leash out of Meg's hand.

"He spotted his brother!" Charlie said with a laugh. He pointed to another ball of golden fur, shooting out from under the

BREAD

MUFFINS

Cocina Mexicana stall, which was run by their friend Juan. Juan's puppy, Paco, was wagging his tail so hard that it was a blur.

"Woof, woof, woof!" The two puppies pounced gleefully on each other and rolled over and over, toppling a sack of sweet potatoes.

"Oops!" Meg murmured. She untangled Buster's leash and picked up the potatoes.

"Oh, that's no problem," said Juan. His face lit up in a huge grin. "I love to see Paco play with Buster. I played with my brother like that when we were small, too!"

Meg and Charlie laughed.

"Buster looks great," Juan went on. "I guess he likes living with you at Pet Hotel."

"He loves it!" Meg said happily.

"Buster gets along with all the guests," Charlie said. "Even the cats!"

"That's good to hear," Juan said, unpacking a box of pineapples. "Have a great day, you two. Thanks for stopping by!"

"See you later," Meg and Charlie called, waving good-bye. They walked across the street to a tall old brownstone with a freshly painted front door. Above the door was a big new sign that read PET HOTEL.

Meg and Charlie both looked up at the sign and beamed from ear to ear. When

they'd first arrived at Gazebo Square, their
great-great-aunt Saffron's hotel had been a
regular hotel for people, but it was so run-
down that it didn't have any guests. When
Juan had hurt his ankle, Meg and Charlie
had taken care of Paco — and realized that
the hotel made a perfect place for pets to
stay. It was already an amazing success!
Right now, their guests were six goldfish,

two cats, three dogs, a rabbit, four guinea pigs, and a —

"Wheeeeep!" An ear-piercing screech came from inside the hotel, making Charlie, Meg, and Buster leap into the air.

Meg held tightly to Buster's leash and carefully pushed open the sky-blue door.

"Wheee-wheee-wheeep!" The noise was coming from upstairs.

Charlie shut the hotel door firmly behind them so that none of the pets could get out.

There was another screech, as loud as a train coming into a station.

Meg giggled as she hung Buster's leash on a peg beside the front door. "Any second now, the singing will start," she said.

Charlie quickly clapped his hands over his ears.

Sure enough, a voice echoed down the stairs: *"You ain't nothing but a hound dog! You ain't nothing but a hound dog!"* It sounded like an opera singer being strangled.

Buster threw back his head. *"Aooo-ooo!"* he howled.

"Elvis is awake," Meg said. She and Charlie dropped their basket and backpack on the reception desk and raced upstairs to see their latest guest.

CHAPTER 2

Meg pushed open the door to her room. On her desk was a large cage, and inside the cage was Elvis — a gray-and-white cockatiel with pumpkin-orange cheeks and a bright yellow head crest.

"You ain't nothing but a hound dog! You ain't nothing but a hound dog!" Elvis screeched over and over again.

"Morning, Elvis!" Charlie opened the door to the birdcage. The little cockatiel had spent the night safely locked up, but he was so tame that he was allowed to roam around the hotel during the day. Elvis hopped onto Charlie's shoulder and gently nibbled his ear.

"We'll play later, Elvis," Meg promised. "But right now we need to give the other guests their breakfast." She scooped Elvis off Charlie's shoulder and gently lowered him to the floor.

Elvis strutted after the twins as they headed downstairs. He followed quietly behind, hopping down each step. Meg and Charlie carried their basket and backpack into the kitchen, where Mom and Saffron were finishing their breakfast.

Saffron's crinkled face lit up when they came in. She was wearing a purple flower in her long silver hair and a dress patterned with orange sunbursts.

"Let me help, my dears." The bells on Saffron's earrings jingled as she rose slowly to her feet.

"Did you get everything?" Mom asked the twins, leading the way into the old pantry, which had been converted into a special kitchen for preparing pet food.

"I have dry dog and cat food. . . ." Meg said, tipping it into individual bowls. Buster sat beside her feet, drooling.

Charlie pulled things out of his backpack and piled them on the table. "Pellets for the rabbit, guinea pig mix, sunflower seeds for treats, fish flakes . . ."

". . . and some delicious fruit," added Saffron, peering into the backpack and pulling out a bunch of grapes.

Just then, there was a strange *click-click-click*ing noise outside the door. Buster's furry ears perked up.

"Is that a mouse?" Mom asked suspiciously.

"Wheep!" The whistle was followed by another rattle of claws on the tiled floor. Elvis skittered into the pet kitchen, bobbing his head up and down and raising his yellow crest so that it stood up like a Mohawk. Buster tilted his head to one side and looked at Elvis in amazement.

"I read that cockatiels put up their crests when they're excited," Charlie noted, as Elvis's bright, beady eyes surveyed the room.

"Tuk . . . tuk . . . tuk . . ." The little cockatiel made a clicking sound with his beak and strutted around the kitchen, weaving between Meg's and Charlie's legs. He stopped behind Buster. Before Buster had time to figure out what was happening, Elvis hopped onto his tail, walked up his back, and jumped off the puppy's head onto a kitchen chair!

"Woof!" Buster barked, shaking himself from nose to tail. He was clearly surprised at being used as a stepladder.

Elvis looked up longingly at the fruit on the table and whistled as loudly as he could.

"It's a shame he won't fly anymore," Saffron commented between the barks, whistles, and laughter.

The twins looked at each other. Now that they thought about it, they'd never seen Elvis fly — he hopped everywhere!

"What's the matter with him?" Charlie asked.

"Elvis's owner, Anton, told me that Elvis stopped flying after he hurt his wing,"

Saffron explained. "It's completely healed now, but he still doesn't want to use it."

"Maybe he's forgotten how to fly," Meg suggested.

"Or he's scared to try," Charlie added. Then his eyes lit up. "Maybe we can help him fly again!"

CHAPTER 3

Dad poked his head around the old pantry door.

"What's all the barking and squawking about?" he asked. The twins explained Elvis's clever climbing trick and how they wanted to help him learn to fly again.

"Great idea — but let's get breakfast out of the way first," Dad told them with a smile.

Meg scooped Elvis up and gently tickled the back of his neck before setting him down on the table.

"Wheep!" Elvis whistled, *click-clack*ing along the table toward the fruit bowl. He pecked at the cat food along the way, then sank his beak into a grape. Juice ran down his chin, and he made gleeful sounds as he nibbled.

"Well, Elvis's breakfast is all taken care of," Mom said with a laugh.

Meg couldn't help laughing at the little bird. "We'll take breakfast to the other guests," she said.

The twins loaded the pets' food into the crate-sized elevator that Saffron called a dumbwaiter. Meg yanked on the rope and hoisted it up to the second floor.

As she did, Charlie ran up the stairs, opened the dumbwaiter hatch, and pulled out two bowls. He headed to the guest room for cats, which was decorated to look like ancient Egypt. The room had statues of pharaohs near the fireplace, plus six pens with scratching posts shaped like palm trees. A pair of loud meows welcomed him.

"Good morning!" Charlie greeted Smudge and Cookie, the kitty guests, as they pushed their heads against the bars to be stroked.

He set the bowls of cat food in the pen, and the room filled with contented purrs and munching. Charlie beamed. Cats were his favorite animals, and whenever he had time he went to the Egyptian room to pet them and play. Cat fishing with a feather on a string was the best game ever! Smudge and Cookie were really good at it, but soon they would be going home.

"I wish I had a cat of my very own that I never had to say good-bye to." Charlie sighed as he shut the door.

Down the hall, Meg carried a tray of bowls into a room that had been painted to look like a forest. Buddy the boxer, Daisy the West Highland white terrier, and Max the dachshund were ready for their breakfast. There was a chorus of happy woofs when Meg opened the door! Buddy began to drool, Daisy jumped up and down, and Max waggled his long body from nose to tail.

"I'll be back later to groom you and take you for a walk," Meg promised the three doggie guests as they gobbled down their food.

Once the dogs and cats had been fed, the twins met back at the dumbwaiter.

"My turn!" said Charlie. He tugged on the rope until the little elevator reached the fourth floor, then he and Meg raced up the stairs to meet it. The rest of the break-fasts were for the guests in the old playroom, which had been converted to look like a summer meadow.

The guinea pigs snuffled a greeting as Meg fed them and checked to make sure that their water bottle was full. Charlie put a dish full of pellets into the rabbit run, then picked some fresh dandelion leaves from the wooden trough under the window. Clover the rabbit wiggled her nose in delight.

"It's fun feeding our littlest guests!" Meg commented as she held out a dandelion stalk to a red-eyed guinea pig named Ruby. She smiled as Ruby nibbled it up like a string of spaghetti.

They'd just finished giving the pets their breakfast when the hotel doorbell rang.

"NEW GUEST!" Meg and Charlie shouted together.

They rushed downstairs as Mom answered the door. It was Carmen, who ran the cupcake stall at the farmers' market. She was carrying a box in one hand and a cat carrier in the other. Buster bounded up to the door, wagging his tail in greeting.

"Good morning!" Carmen smiled, handing the box to Charlie. "Some cupcakes for you all, as thanks for watching Matilda," she said.

"Ooh, thanks!" Meg and Charlie exclaimed. They crouched down to greet the big tabby cat in the carrier as Mom checked the booking on the computer. Charlie tried to tickle the cat through the bars, but Matilda turned away.

"She's staying for one night while I go to my cousin's wedding," Carmen was explaining. "But I'm worried about leaving her. About a month ago she started getting chubby — and yesterday I gave her a new catnip mouse, and she didn't want to play with it. That's not like Matilda at all."

"We'll take good care of her," Charlie reassured Carmen.

"It's fun to stay at Pet Hotel," Meg added. "Maybe she'll make friends with another guest. That will cheer her up!"

CHAPTER 4

Mom and the twins waved good-bye to Carmen. Charlie closed the door just as Elvis strutted into the reception area.

"I guess he smelled the cupcakes!" Meg giggled.

But Elvis ignored the cupcakes and walked right up to Matilda's carrier instead. He strutted around it, then peered through the bars and raised his crest.

"*Tuk tuk tuk,*" he muttered, bobbing his head up and down. "*Tuk tuk tuk...*" Using his beak and claws, he pulled himself up the wire on the front of the carrier, scrambled up on top, then bent his head down so that he could see Matilda sitting inside.

"*TUK!*" he announced cheerily.

Charlie picked up the carrier.

Elvis lowered his crest and gave an angry squawk as he hopped down.

"Elvis didn't want you to move Matilda," Meg said as they brought the tabby's carrier upstairs to the cat guest room. "I think he likes her!"

Charlie put Matilda's carrier down in the pen next to Cookie's and opened the door at the front. Cookie meowed a welcome.

"Come on out, Matilda," Charlie said.

But there was a hissing noise from inside the carrier.

The twins peered in. Matilda was hunkered down at the very back.

"I don't think she wants to make friends," Meg commented.

"If she's having a tough week, maybe she just needs peace and quiet," Charlie said thoughtfully. "Let's see if she likes it next door, in the box room."

He closed the door to the carrier and brought it into a small room lined with suitcases, packing crates, and old boxes. The twins put Matilda's carrier in a quiet corner, then went to get food, water, and a litter box.

"Here you go, Matilda. Your own private hotel suite," Meg joked when they came back. She opened the door to the travel carrier again. The big gray-and-brown cat looked up at her and blinked — but didn't budge.

"I know!" said Charlie suddenly. "I bet some treats will tempt her out." He ran downstairs to grab a packet of Kitty Krunchies, then made a trail of treats leading from the carrier when he got back upstairs. First Matilda's nose poked out, sniffing, then the rest of her slowly emerged. Her big belly hung almost to the floor.

"I love her stripy fur," Meg murmured as Matilda gobbled up the trail of treats.

"After this, we'll cheer her up by playing some games," Charlie whispered. But as soon as Matilda finished eating, she turned and slunk back to her travel carrier.

"Maybe she's upset about something," Meg suggested.

"We need to take her mind off it, then," Charlie said. "But how?"

The twins were silent for a moment.

"Remember when Paco ran away to the Pet Bakery?" Meg said. "There was one thing that took his mind off all those dog cookies...."

"Saffron's feather boa!" said Charlie. "Maybe Matilda will like it, too!"

He rushed off again and came back with the turquoise feather boa — and Elvis perched on his wrist.

"Look who was hopping up the stairs!" Charlie said, lowering his arm so that the cockatiel could jump to the floor. "I guess he was trying to find Matilda."

Sure enough, Elvis squawked happily when he saw Matilda's travel carrier.

"You ain't nothing but a hound dog!" he screeched.

"Matilda's a cat, not a hound dog," Meg joked.

"You ain't nothing but a hound dog!" Elvis hopped toward the carrier. Inside, Matilda flattened her ears. Meg quickly scooped Elvis away. Elvis stopped singing and looked over at the tabby, his head tilted to one side.

"I'm not sure Matilda wants to be friends right now," Meg told Elvis gently.

The cockatiel's beady eyes watched as Charlie wriggled the boa along the floor in front of the carrier. Matilda squeezed out again and sniffed at the turquoise feathers.

She lifted her head and looked around the room.

"It's working!" Meg whispered to Charlie.

But Matilda just gave a mournful cry. *"Meee-ow!"* She walked past the feather boa, headed for a dark, cozy-looking space between two suitcases, and curled up.

"Maybe she'd rather play with a cat toy." Charlie rushed off to the Egyptian room and came back with a feather on a string, a catnip mouse, and a Ping-Pong ball. But Matilda ignored those, too.

"She's acting so strange," Meg said. Her forehead creased in a worried frown. "Why can't we cheer her up?"

CHAPTER 5

"There's one last thing we can try," Charlie announced. "Cats love to climb. We can make an obstacle course for Matilda!"

"Great idea!" Meg agreed, carefully setting Elvis down by the door. The twins piled up suitcases and boxes around the room, making little staircases and slopes, bridges to race across, and a high platform to sit on.

"Wheep!" Elvis raised his crest and ran

across the floor. He skittered up one of the slopes, bobbing his head.

"Well, Elvis likes it!" Charlie laughed. But it wasn't the cockatiel they were trying to impress.

"Your turn, Matilda," Meg announced. Matilda just blinked and wriggled farther into her cozy space.

"Maybe she thinks the obstacle course is just for birds," suggested Charlie. "Buster could show her that it's fun for furry animals, too. . . ."

"Buster might scare her," Meg pointed out.

"Matilda looks so fed up," Charlie said with a sigh. "It's worth a try."

Meg shrugged and opened the door. "Buster!" she yelled.

Immediately, the furry little puppy hurtled up the stairs and shot into the room. He took one look at the obstacle course and bounded up onto it, wagging his tail and yapping with excitement. When he reached the top, Matilda flattened her ears and gave a loud howl. *"MEEEOOOW!"*

Buster leaped off the suitcase in surprise. When he did, the suitcase wobbled and fell to the floor with its lid open.

Matilda suddenly sprang into action. She jumped inside the suitcase and began to knead at the lining with her front paws, circling around. Then she lay down with her back to the twins.

"I think she wants to be left alone," Charlie said.

"Maybe she just needs a rest," Meg agreed.

They shooed Buster and Elvis out into the hall, quietly closed the door to Matilda's room, and went downstairs.

⊱ ⊰ ⊱

"My dears, it's time to walk the dogs!" Saffron announced after lunch.

"I'll go get them," said Meg. She hurried upstairs while Charlie went to fill his backpack with plastic bags, a water bottle, and a bowl from the pet kitchen.

"There's only one grape left on the bunch we bought this morning!" Charlie said to Saffron as he filled his water bottle at the sink.

"Elvis keeps sneaking in and stealing them. He loves grapes." Saffron smiled, clipping Buster's leash to his collar.

There was a rumbling noise as Meg thundered downstairs with an avalanche of eager dogs. They skidded to a stop at the front door.

"You take Max and Daisy," she said, handing Charlie their leashes. "Saffron can take Buster, and I'll take Buddy." The big boxer gave her hand a slobbery lick.

Four tails wagged as Saffron opened the door.

"What fun!" Saffron smiled as Buster pulled her toward the nearby park, weaving between the bustling stalls of Gazebo Square and under the old archway.

In the park, Saffron took a seat on her

favorite bench and handed Buster's leash to Meg. Charlie dropped his backpack at their great-great-aunt's feet.

"It's like being pulled by a team of huskies!" Meg joked as she and Charlie ran around the park with the dogs on their leashes.

They were all panting by the time they got back to Saffron. Meg and Charlie sat down next to her and poured water into the dogs' bowl.

"I wish Matilda had this much energy," Charlie puffed as the dogs lapped up the water.

"Matilda who?" Saffron asked.

"Carmen's tabby cat," Charlie explained. "Carmen's worried about her because she's gained a lot of weight and is in a cranky mood. We're trying to cheer her up."

"All she wants to do is find a cozy little space and sit in it," Meg added.

Saffron's eyes twinkled. "It sounds like Matilda's making a nest," she remarked.

"Why would a cat want to make a nest?" Meg asked. She looked up as a sparrow flew past, its beak full of dried grass. "Birds make nests . . ."

". . . to lay their eggs in!" finished Charlie. His mouth dropped open.

The twins looked at each other.

"Oh!" they exclaimed together.

"So that's why Matilda's tummy is so big!" Meg gasped.

"She's going to have kittens!" Charlie grinned. "Awesome!"

"When I was in Morocco," Saffron said with a faraway look in her eyes, "I helped a mother cat who was about to have kittens. The only quiet place I could find for her was inside my backpack." She looked at the twins and smiled. "I think you've got time to make Matilda a nice birthing box."

"We need to get back right now!" Charlie cried.

Saffron nodded. "Go — I'll catch up with you!"

Meg and Charlie sprinted back to the hotel, with the dogs bounding beside them. They quickly settled the doggie guests back in their pens, and Buster scampered after them as they hurried to Matilda's room. There was a white feather on the floor outside — and the door was open.

"Elvis! How did he get in?" Meg wondered.

But inside the room, there was no sign of Elvis — or Matilda.

"Oh, no!" Charlie groaned. "Matilda disappeared!"

"We have to find her!" Meg said. "She's about to have kittens — and she needs our help!"

CHAPTER 6

"MATILDA!" Charlie called. The twins and Buster raced around the hotel, peering under beds and looking inside drawers. The dogs woofed, Smudge and Cookie meowed, and the rabbit and guinea pigs scampered around in circles, but Carmen's tabby cat was nowhere to be seen.

"What about the laundry basket?" Meg suggested, panting. "Matilda might have made a nest inside it."

They ran down to the basement, but the laundry basket was empty. Buster's tail drooped.

Charlie scratched his head. "Matilda can't have disappeared into thin air," he muttered. "She *has* to be somewhere in the hotel!"

"We should look for Elvis," said Meg. "He keeps following her around, so he might be with her now. . . ."

Buster perked up his ears and tilted his head to one side. *"Aooo!"* he howled softly.

"I think he can hear something," Charlie said. The twins listened carefully.

From somewhere above them came the faint sound of muffled, echoey singing. *"You ain't nothing but a hound dog!"*

"Elvis!" Charlie cried. "But he sounds all closed in, like he's *inside* something."

The twins followed the sound into the kitchen.

"He's inside the wall!" Meg said, looking around in confusion. "But where?"

Buster dashed toward the dumbwaiter. He stopped and sniffed.

Charlie put his ear to the closed hatch.

"Elvis is in the dumbwaiter shaft!" he declared. "He must have found an open hatch, hopped in, and gotten stuck."

"Why would he want to go in there?" Meg asked. "It's dark and —"

"— cozy, like a nest!" Charlie added excitedly. "Elvis really likes Matilda, right? Maybe she's inside the dumbwaiter, too!"

He opened the hatch. Carefully peering in, he twisted his head to look up the shaft.

"It's stopped at the second floor," he reported.

They sped upstairs. The hatch was open, and there was Matilda, huddled inside the small metal elevator, right at the back. The twins breathed a sigh of relief.

Matilda's fur rippled in surprise, and she gave a loud meow.

"You ain't nothing but a hound dog!" Elvis squawked from above. He sounded much closer than before.

Meg gulped. "Elvis must be sitting right on top of the dumbwaiter!" she said. "What should we do? He'll bother Matilda, and she needs peace and quiet!"

Saffron appeared at the top of the stairs, just back from the park.

"First things first, my dears," she announced. "We need to help Matilda make a comfy nest. You'll find an old blanket in the laundry room, some newspaper in the kitchen, and a shallow cardboard box in Matilda's room."

The twins hurried off to get everything. Saffron nodded approvingly as they lined the box with the blanket and newspaper and gently placed it inside the dumbwaiter.

"Meow!" Matilda clambered awkwardly inside the box and started to shred the newspaper with her claws.

"Why is she doing that?" Meg asked.

"She's making a lining for her nest, so it's exactly how she wants it," Saffron explained.

When the newspaper was a heap of narrow strips, Matilda circled around and around in it. She settled for a moment, then shifted and began to purr.

"I'm surprised she's purring!" Charlie

whispered. "She doesn't look very comfortable."

"She's calming herself," Saffron murmured, placing a bowl of food and a saucer of water next to Matilda's nest.

"You ain't nothing but a hound dog!" Elvis screeched from above.

"Aooo-ooo!" Buster joined in.

Matilda got to her feet and arched her back. *"Sssss!"* she hissed.

"What Matilda needs now is quiet," Saffron said calmly to the twins.

"*Shhhh!*" Meg told Buster, and he stopped howling.

"That's better, but we can't shush Elvis," Charlie said. "We have to get him out of there!"

But how could they get the little cockatiel out of the elevator shaft if he refused to fly?

"I'll stay with Matilda," Saffron told Charlie and Meg. "You go and rescue that silly birdie." She sat cross-legged on the floor next to the dumbwaiter, humming softly to herself.

The twins could hear Elvis squawking as they hurried to the floor above, with Buster close behind. Charlie opened the hatch to the dumbwaiter. They peered down the gloomy shaft.

Elvis was hopping around on top of the elevator. His white feathers seemed to glow in the dim light.

"Aooo-ooo!" Buster rose up on his hind legs, trying to peer down the elevator shaft.

"I think you'd better stay out of the way until this is over," Meg told him. "Come on." The little puppy trotted after her as she led the way to her bedroom. She pointed to a big, floppy cushion on the floor. Buster curled up on it and gave a huge puppy yawn. "Good boy!" Meg patted his head. Then she closed the door and went back to the dumb-waiter hatch.

"Elvis!" Charlie called. The little cocka-tiel glanced up at him.

"Come on, buddy — fly!" Meg encouraged him, but Elvis just bobbed his head. "We could pull the dumbwaiter up," she suggested.

"That would bother Matilda even more," Charlie pointed out. "We have to get Elvis to *fly* out."

"Hey, what about grapes?" Meg said excitedly after a minute. "He loves grapes! Let's try it. . . ."

CHAPTER 7

Meg ran downstairs and grabbed the bunch, with its one remaining grape, from the kitchen, then hurried back and dangled it through the hatch.

Elvis stopped singing and raised his crest, then opened his beak and squawked.

Meg groaned. "He expects me to drop it in his mouth!" She waved the grape at Elvis. "You have to fly up and get it!"

Elvis closed his beak and fluttered his wings.

"That's it!" Meg jiggled the grape again. Elvis flapped his wings faster, and for a moment his feet left the top of the dumbwaiter. He landed again, looking surprised.

"You can do it!" Charlie called.

Elvis flapped his wings faster and faster and faster. . . .

All of a sudden, he took off and flew up the dumbwaiter shaft and out of the hatch!

"Wheep!" whistled the little cockatiel as he soared over the twins' heads.

"Go, Elvis!" Meg and Charlie cheered.

Meg ran down the hall and dangled the grape in front of her bedroom door.

"Here you go, Elvis! You can keep Buster company," she told the cockatiel. Meg went into her bedroom and laid the grape on the bottom of Elvis's open cage. He swooped inside and settled on his perch to nibble the grape, chattering happily. On the other side of the room, Buster's eyes opened for a moment before he went back to sleep.

Charlie peeked through the door. "Everything's finally nice and quiet!" he said with a sigh of relief.

Closing Meg's door gently behind them, the twins tiptoed downstairs. Saffron was still sitting cross-legged on the floor. She had her hands in her lap and her eyes closed.

"Has Matilda had her kittens yet?" Charlie whispered.

Saffron opened her eyes. "These things take time," she murmured calmly. "All we can do now is wait. . . ." She shut her eyes again.

It was very, very hard to wait. Charlie took all of his cat books into Meg's room and tried to read everything he could find about kittens, but it was tough to concentrate. Meg watched Elvis as he flew around the room, pausing every so often to perch on the lampshade and whistle.

On the cushion next to Charlie, Buster snored. "That's the best way to pass the time," Charlie said, smiling at the little puppy.

Meg nodded. "But I couldn't sleep right now — I'm too excited!"

"Matilda did it!" Saffron called at last.

"YES!" the twins shouted, running into the hall.

"Wheeeep!" Elvis whistled.

Buster jumped to his feet with an excited bark.

They all tore downstairs and met Mom and Dad on the second-floor landing. A loud purr was coming from inside the dumb-waiter — and a soft chorus of squeaky little meows.

"The kittens have been born!" Saffron confirmed. The flower in her hair was drooping, but she was beaming from ear to ear.

Meg and Charlie peered inside the dumbwaiter.

"Awww!" they breathed.

Five tiny, pink-nosed kittens were snuggled up to Matilda. She was licking them from nose to tail, purring happily. All of the kittens looked completely different! One was a tabby like Matilda, one was orange, one was black with a white marking on its chest, one was cream and gray, and the smallest was covered in black and white splotches. It had one black ear and one white ear, and a stripy black-and-white tail.

"Their eyes are squeezed shut and their ears are all crumply," Meg whispered.

"That's because they're so new," Charlie explained, his eyes sparkling. "The books say it takes a couple of weeks for their eyes and ears to open." He could hardly believe his luck. Kittens born at Pet Hotel!

"I'll make sure they're all okay," Dad said, gently scooping up a damp kitten. He dabbed it with a towel and checked it over before putting it back with Matilda.

"Look at their little claws and whiskers," Meg said adoringly as Dad checked each one carefully. "They're *purr*-fect!"

"They are," Mom agreed with a grin.

"Take a look, Buster!" Meg held on to

the puppy's collar while he snuffled at the new family and wagged his tail.

Just then, Elvis swooped down onto Charlie's shoulder. *"Tuk tuk tuk!"* he chirped, fluffing up his crest and flapping his wings with excitement.

"Yes, you have six kitty friends now!" Meg said with a giggle.

Matilda looked up at them and purred contentedly.

"Carmen's in for a surprise," Charlie said.

"Five surprises!" joked Meg.

"We should leave Matilda to feed her kittens in peace," Saffron advised. "She's worn out by all the excitement."

"It's definitely been an exciting day at Pet Hotel!" Charlie agreed as they all tiptoed downstairs.

CHAPTER 8

Carmen's mouth fell open in amazement when Mom and Dad told her the news the next day.

"Kittens?!" she gasped.

"Come and see!" Charlie and Meg led the way to the dumbwaiter. Matilda and her kittens looked very comfortable in their warm, cozy nest.

"Oh, my goodness!" Carmen murmured. "What a funny girl you are, Matilda." She paused for a minute. "But I'm not ready to look after *six* cats. . . ."

"Matilda and her kittens are welcome to stay at Pet Hotel for the next couple of weeks," Mom told her.

"I read that the kittens' eyes and ears will be open by then," Charlie added.

Carmen's face lit up. "That's so nice of you," she said. "It will give me time to get things ready — and to start finding them all good homes."

"They'll be ready to leave their mom when they're twelve weeks old," Charlie told her.

He gently picked up the tiny black-and-white kitten. It nestled, warm and soft, in the palm of his hand. A loving feeling washed over Charlie as the kitten pushed its head against his fingers and gave a tiny squeak.

Carmen beamed at Charlie. "Someone who knows all about kittens would make a great owner," she said.

"You definitely need someone who knows about litter boxes and scratching posts and toys," Charlie agreed.

"Someone like you," Carmen added with a wink. "Sounds like I've found an ideal home for one lucky little black-and-white kitten! How about it, Mom and Dad?"

Charlie and Meg both looked up in surprise and held their breath.

"Of course!" Dad said, ruffling Charlie's hair.

"Awesome!" the twins cheered under their breath, trying not to disturb the kittens.

At that moment, the doorbell rang. Mom and Dad went down to answer it, and reappeared with a teenage boy wearing a T-shirt with a picture of a guitar on the front.

Dad introduced everyone. "Anton's here to pick up Elvis, but I thought he'd like to see Matilda and her newborn kittens first."

Anton grinned as he peered into the dumbwaiter. "Cool!" he said. "They're so cute!"

There was an excited *"Wheep!"* and Elvis swooped down the stairs, looped around Anton, and settled on his shoulder.

"You can fly again!" Anton exclaimed as the cockatiel nibbled at his ear, making happy sounds.

Elvis hopped off Anton's shoulder onto the sill of the dumbwaiter, then strutted inside. Anton's mouth fell open as Elvis carefully picked his way around the kittens and snuggled up among them, next to Matilda.

"He loves Matilda," Charlie explained. "He helped us find her when she hid in here to have her kittens."

Anton peered thoughtfully at the happy scene inside the dumbwaiter. "Carmen?" he asked slowly. "Would it be okay for me to ask my parents if I can adopt this little

kitten when it's old enough? The one with the white patch?"

"That would be wonderful!" Carmen said.

Anton grinned. "Then Elvis will have a new friend."

Meg went to get the little cockatiel's cage from her room.

"Thank you for taking such good care of him while I was gone," Anton said as he carefully placed Elvis on the perch in his cage and closed the door. Mom and Dad led him downstairs.

There was an extra-loud whistle as the front door opened. *You ain't nothing but a hound dog!* Elvis screeched before the door closed again.

"Elvis has left the building!" Dad called up the stairs. Everyone giggled.

"Hey!" Charlie said, his eyes lighting up. "How about we name the kittens after famous musicians?"

"That's a great idea," Carmen agreed. "We could do Ella for Ella Fitzgerald, Duke for Duke Ellington, Judy for Judy Holliday . . ."

"Dylan for Bob Dylan, and Woody for Woody Guthrie," Saffron added eagerly. "They're my favorites!"

Meg and Charlie looked at each other, confused. Who?

"I'll play you some of their music later," Saffron said with a laugh, "and tell you about the time I met Bob Dylan."

"I like 'Woody' best," Charlie declared. "That's what I'm going to name my kitten!"

Two weeks passed quickly, and soon it was time for the cat family to go home with Carmen. Matilda and four of her kittens were already in the carrier. The kittens' eyes had opened already!

Charlie gently picked up Woody and put him in the carrier, too. The kitten's bright blue eyes blinked up at him.

"Good-bye for now," Charlie said softly. "I'll see you again when you're old enough to leave your mom."

"He'll be back before you know it," Carmen said. "I've found homes for the others with people on Gazebo Square, so you'll see them all again!"

Carmen closed the carrier and carried it carefully downstairs to where Buster was waiting at the front door. She lowered the carrier so that the little puppy could say his good-byes.

"Bye!" called Meg and Charlie, waving.

"It'll be so cool when Woody is big enough to come and live with us," Charlie said to his sister.

"Then we'll have a puppy *and* a kitten," Meg added. "And a hotel full of animal guests! What more could anyone want?"

PET HOTEL

Check out who's checking in —
don't miss the next Pet Hotel book!

Pet Hotel #3: A Nose for Trouble

CHAPTER 1

Charlie sat upright in bed with a start. His room was filled with a strange rumbling, whirring noise.

"What's that?" he exclaimed, turning on the light. The elephants, hippos, lions, and tigers on his wallpaper seemed to stare back at him.

Whirrr-zzz-zzz! The strange sound was coming from outside his room.

Could a guest at Pet Hotel be making all that noise? The hotel was almost full of pet guests, for the first time since it had opened. Charlie and his twin sister, Meg, had given their mom and dad the idea to turn Great-Great-Aunt Saffron's old hotel into a pet hotel, and now they were taking care of lots of cats and dogs and small furry pets. But as far as Charlie knew, none of them made this kind of noise. It sounded like a giant mechanical bee!

Charlie leaped out of bed and pulled on his paw-print bathrobe. He cautiously opened the door. Two shining lights, like eyes, were coming toward him down the hall.

Tingles ran up and down Charlie's spine . . . but it was only Meg, shining her pig-shaped flashlight at him. The two spots of light were coming out of its snout!

"What's making that noise?" Meg asked in a whisper.

"I don't know," Charlie murmured. "We'd better check on our guests."

They tiptoed down the stairs to the second floor, where the cats and dogs slept.

"The noise isn't as loud down here," Meg said softly as they peered into the Egyptian room, which had been turned into a special guest room for cats. The statues of pharaohs and the scratching posts in the shape of palm trees made spooky shadows outside the beam of the flashlight. Marmalade was licking her paws and washing behind her ears, and Oreo was stalking a toy mouse.

Ginger, Mabel, Skittles, and Ollie were curled up, fast asleep.

"Cats are the best pets ever." Charlie sighed.

"You'll have your own soon," Meg whispered.

"Very soon!" Charlie grinned. Woody, one of the kittens who had recently been born at Pet Hotel, would be old enough to leave his mother and come back this week! Yesterday, Charlie had helped Mom and Dad set up a brand-new cat basket and litter tray for Woody in the corner of the kitchen. He'd spent all the allowance he'd been saving on kitty toys. Charlie couldn't wait for Woody to come and be his very own pet!

At the other end of the hallway, four of the five dogs staying in the forest room were also snoozing peacefully. Meg shone her flashlight around the dark room. The trees on the wallpaper made it look like a peaceful forest. Affie the Afghan hound and Judy the Old English sheepdog were twitching as they ran in their sleep. Chico the Chihuahua and Amber the Lab were snoring loudly.

"Daisy's awake!" Meg pointed to the West Highland terrier, a frequent guest at Pet Hotel. She had her head tilted to one side as she listened carefully to the strange noise.

"*Woof!*" Daisy barked softly when she saw the twins.

"*Shhhh!*" Meg crept into the room and put her hand between the bars of Daisy's pen to soothe her. She didn't want Daisy to wake up the rest of the dogs! If she started barking, that would wake Mom and Dad and Saffron — and Meg's own puppy, Buster, who slept in his basket downstairs in the kitchen. Daisy licked Meg's hand and trotted back to her bed. Meg joined Charlie, who was creeping silently down the hall.

Zzz-zzz-whirrr . . .

It was hard to figure out where the noise was coming from!

Charlie stopped near the tiny dumbwaiter and put his ear to the hatch.

"It's definitely louder upstairs," he told Meg. "Let's check the guest room in the attic!"

"But there are only little furry animals up there," Meg said. "They're usually so quiet."

The twins tiptoed up the stairs. Charlie opened the door to the old playroom that had been painted to look like a meadow. It was bathed in silvery light from the full moon outside. The twins could see that, in the twelve hutches around the room, all the little animal guests were wide awake! Many of the hutches had more than one pet inside, since the guests had arrived in groups of two or three. The five rabbits were hopping around, the eight gerbils were gnawing at their cereal bars, and the six guinea pigs made whistling noises as Meg and Charlie entered the room.

Whirrr-zzz-zzz . . .

"It's coming from that corner!" Charlie exclaimed, pointing.

They tiptoed across the playroom and stopped by the multistory hamster pen.

"It's Bluebell, Tulip, and Sweet Pea!" Meg gasped, pointing to the three dwarf hamsters who had arrived at the hotel earlier that day. They were running around and around on their exercise wheels, making them go so fast that their little feet were a blur.

Charlie and Meg grinned at each other. Pet Hotel's smallest guests were the ones making the biggest noise!

KITTY CORNER

Where kitties get the love they need

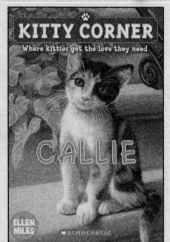

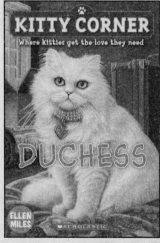
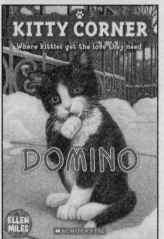